Lesley Ely

was born in Lincolnshire.

She spent several years living and teaching in Africa

before returning to the UK. After the birth of her children

she specialised in teaching English as a foreign language to children

aged 5-9 years and to teenagers. In 1987 she was appointed

head teacher. Louis and his classmates are based

on children whom Lesley has known and taught during her career.

This is Lesley's first book for Frances Lincoln.

Polly Dunbar

was born in Stratford upon Avon.

Daughter of children's author, Joyce Dunbar,

Polly first started illustrating when she was 16

and now has a degree in Illustration from the University of Brighton.

This is Polly's first book for Frances Lincoln.

In memory of Adam and for Richard, with love   L.E.
For Teresa Cole   P.D.

First published in Great Britain in 2004 by Frances Lincoln Children's Books,
4 Torriano Mews, Torriano Avenue, London NW5 2RZ
www.franceslincoln.com

First paperback edition published in 2005

British Library Cataloguing in Publication Data available on request

ISBN 10: 1-84507-083-6
ISBN 13: 978-1-84507-083-0

Set in Avenir

Printed in Singapore

3 5 7 9 8 6 4 2

Looking after Louis

Written by Lesley Ely
Illustrated by Polly Dunbar

F

FRANCES LINCOLN
CHILDREN'S BOOKS

Looking

at —

There's a new boy at school called Louis. Louis sits next to me and I look after him. He's not quite like the rest of us. Sometimes I wonder what he's thinking about. He often just sits and stares at the wall. If I ask him what he's looking at he says, "Looking at," and carries on looking.

I show him my pictures and I say, "Try these crayons, Louis."

He says, "Try these crayons, Louis."

Then he draws very carefully so I say, "That's good."

But I don't know what his pictures are about.

Me and Em look after Louis at playtime. He runs in and out of the boys' football game with his arms out like a ballet dancer.

Me and Em thought he was playing football at first but he wasn't. He just likes running inside the game. The boys get mad but Louis doesn't notice.

Sometimes Miss Owlie says, "No football allowed today,"
and the footballers slouch about and can't think what to do.
Then boys and girls play together for a change.
Last no-football day we let our friend Sam on the big tyre
with us. He wobbled but we didn't laugh.

Louis was standing quite still, just watching, so I called out,
"Do you want to come on the tyre, Louis?"
Louis said, "Come on the tyre, Louis?"
But he didn't move.

Louis sometimes talks in the wrong place.

Yesterday Miss Owlie said, "Sit up straight, everybody."

Louis said, "Sit up straight, everybody."

We all laughed because he sounded just like Miss Owlie. She wasn't cross though. Neither was Mrs Kumar. They would have been cross if me or Em or Sam had done that.

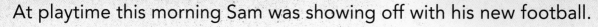

At playtime this morning Sam was showing off with his new football.

Mrs Kumar said, "Sam has magic feet!"

Louis watched Sam's feet closely and Sam tried not to look pleased. He said, "Do you want a game, Louis?"

Louis said, "Game, Louis?"

Sam dribbled the ball all around the playground and Louis ran after him. Sam passed the ball to Louis. Louis didn't get it but Sam kept it going and Louis chased it with his arms out.

Other boys joined in. If Louis' foot even touched the ball, Sam shouted,

"Great game, Louis!"

Louis almost smiled.

Louis drew a picture all afternoon. Every time he used
a different colour he said, "Great game!"

When he'd used every colour, he stopped.

I said, "Show it to Miss Owlie," and I took him to her desk.

I said, "I think Louis' picture is about football."

Miss Owlie looked carefully. "Let's ask the expert!" she said.

So I fetched Sam.

Sam looked at Louis' picture.
Then he said, "That's the game!
That's you! That's me! That's the ball!"
"That's the ball!" said Louis.

That's the ball

Just then the sun shone in.
It shone through the classroom
window.

Sam said, "Shall me and Louis pop outside and practise football again, Miss Owlie?"

Miss Owlie's eyes crinkled up. She said, "Would you like to play football, Louis?"

Play football,
Louis (

Mrs Kumar started to take off her apron and put on her coat.

I think she knew what Louis would say.

"Play football, Louis?" said Louis.

Miss Owlie smiled at Mrs Kumar. "How did we guess?" she said.

Sam and Louis WHOOSHED out of our
classroom like water down a plughole!
Mrs Kumar followed them. She had a ball
in her pocket already.

"You NEVER let US play outside when it's not playtime," I said.
Miss Owlie was smiling but I wasn't smiling. Not even a little bit.
I put my hands on my hips.

"Sam and Louis are lucky ducks today, Miss Owlie," I said.

Miss Owlie's eyes twinkled and she got dimples in both cheeks.

"So they are," she whispered. "What do you think about it?"

She looked at me as if she expected my answer
to be very wise. So I thought extra hard before
I whispered back, "I think we're allowed to break rules
for special people."

Miss Owlie put her finger to her lips and nodded
a tiny little nod that nobody saw but me.

We peeped through the classroom window at Sam
and Louis' Great Game...

and I felt special too.

Everyone is unique. We have things that we are good at and things we find difficult. Louis has an Autistic Spectrum Disorder. This means that he has difficulty with social interaction, social communication and imagination. Each person with an Autistic Spectrum Disorder is different but all will have difficulties in these areas.

People with an Autistic Spectrum Disorder benefit from education that is designed to meet their individual needs. Louis sometimes repeats words he has heard others use because he is trying to make sense of what they have said to him. This is how he learns what words mean and how to use them. Louis would like to join the other children in playing football but he needs some help to learn how to play and to learn the rules. Sometimes Louis finds it difficult to know what he should be concentrating on in the classroom and things that are outside the window can distract him. Louis receives help from Mrs Kumar so that he knows what he is doing in the classroom.

Louis is taught in a mainstream school. His classmates help him to communicate and they learn how to respect the differences of others. Louis' classmates are getting to know him, to know what he likes and what he doesn't like, and this helps them to understand Louis and what makes him special.

ALISON STEWART
Chartered Psychologist, Senior Specialist Speech and Language Therapist.

For further information about Autistic Spectrum Disorders, please contact:
The National Autistic Society, 393 City Road, London, EC1V 1NG, Tel: 020 7833 2299
In Australia, please visit Autism Australia at www.autismaus.com.au

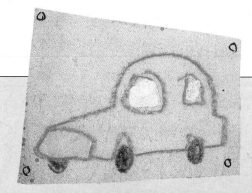

Private and Confidential

Marion Ripley

Illustrated by Colin Backhouse

When Laura gets a letter from Malcolm,
her new Australian penfriend, she is very excited and shows his letter to all her friends.
But when the letters stop, Laura discovers that Malcolm is blind,
and she must learn how to write to him in a different way.
Complete with a braille letter and alphabet card, this is the perfect way
to introduce children to the subject of visual impairment.

ISBN 1-84507-051-8

Lovely Old Roly

Michael Rosen

Illustrated by Priscilla Lamont

Nothing is the same without Roly, the old cat.
The children don't feel like playing their usual games. But then a new cat comes to stay –
a sausage on legs – who slowly makes herself a place in the family.
A sensitive and gentle story about the loss
of a much-loved pet.

ISBN 0-7112-1489-1

Amazing Grace

Mary Hoffman

Illustrated by Caroline Binch

Grace loves to act out stories, so when there's the chance
to play a part in Peter Pan, she longs to play Peter. But her classmates say that Peter
was a boy, and besides, he wasn't black. With the support of her mother
and grandmother, however, Grace soon discovers that if you set your mind to it,
you can do anything you want.

ISBN 0-7112-0699-6

Frances Lincoln titles are available from all good bookshops.
You can also buy books and find out more about your favourite titles, authors
and illustrators on our website: www.franceslincoln.com